The Boy Who Cried Can't!

Thank You

The Boy Who Cried Can't!

by Camesha B. Jackson

Illustrations by Antonio Lee

Dedicated to Grandma Ann, family, and to

all children that have ever cried CAN'T.

–C.B.J

"No, I can't play that game!"

"I can't read this book!

"I can't sweep the floor!

"And I can't even tie my shoes in a perfect bow!"

Whether it was in school, playing with friends, or even at home, Chris felt that he could never be good at anything.

The end of third grade was coming sooner than Chris could imagine. He had totally convinced himself that he couldn't do anything as great as the others around him.

It was one of those real hot sunny days during recess, which meant a perfect day for everyone's favorite playground game, dodge ball. Sara, Chris' friend, quickly ran over to choose him as a teammate, but before Sara could open her lips, Chris belted, "I CAN'T PLAY DODGEBALL!"

Puzzled by his response, Sara said, "Of course you can Chris, everybody knows how to play dodge ball, don't you? Sara hesitated.

"No, I CAN'T!" yelled Chris and off he went.

Later that evening, he was told to clean his room, but as usual he responded, "I CAN'T, Lilly always cleans her room better than me. Mom let's face it, I will never be as good as her." He said sadly.

"You should at least try doing it before saying you can't. I'm sure you will be just as great!" Said his mom.

Now, I know what you may be thinking. Chris wasn't lazy or just using his little sister as an excuse to not clean his room. But the truth is he figured there was no use of trying if he couldn't do it as well as her.

Another dreadful school day Chris thought to himself as he doodled on the back of his notebook.

"Class let's review this week's vocabulary words. Lisa, can you spell rewind? Asked Mrs. J.

"rewind, r-e-w-i-n-d, rewind, " Lisa spoke carefully.

"Wow, such a wonderful speller!" Mrs. J praised.

She slowly began scanning the room looking for her next target. Tick, Tick, Tick, Tick, it was like waiting for a firecracker to pop. Chris knew she could choose him at any moment, so he quietly waited hoping he wouldn't be the next victim. Suddenly, her laser eyes met Chris' with fright. POP!!

As Mrs. J fixed her lips to call on Chris, "I CAN'T spell it!" He blurted.

"Ha, Ha, Ha," all the children laughed at the aftermath of this horrible explosion.

Puzzled Mrs. J. replied, "But I haven't asked you anything yet."

With a cringed mouth he said, "I didn't need to hear it because I can't spell."

Chris' reply never seemed to change especially when his teacher asked him a question. He wasn't as quick as the others, so he didn't feel smart at all. Chris refused to try anything. He couldn't take the chance of being embarrassed.

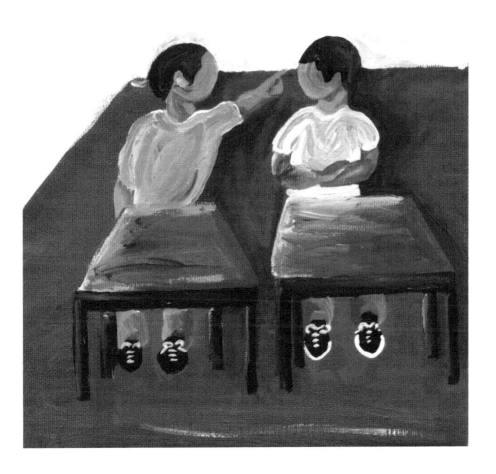

"You can't be afraid to try, bravery is about asking questions and letting everyone know that it's okay to think," Mrs. J spoke firmly.

"I just CAN"T. I CAN'T ask questions in front of the class. They will laugh at me!" Chris said.

She tried, but it was no convincing Chris otherwise.

After some thinking, Chris made up his mind that if he told everyone he couldn't do it, then maybe they would get so mad and never ask him to do anything ever again! He scratched his head, smiling at the clever idea.

As the weeks passed Chris did a great job at being invisible to everyone, except his teacher. Mrs. J was determined to get him out of his shell.   She began noticing drawings on the back of his homework. She didn't know exactly how to react, but it most certainly took her by surprise. Up until this very moment she thought nothing was able to spark Chris into doing something or ANYTHING for that matter.

Ding, Ding, Ding, the intercom sounded, "Students don't forget the annual school trip to the planetarium is in two weeks! So make sure your projects are out of this world!" Principal Huggs eagerly said.

Sirens and trumpets began to play in Chris' head. Sounds of happiness and joy rang clear as day! Little did Mrs. J know this would be the only time Chris would actually be excited about school.

"Remember class your solar system projects are due next week!" Mrs. J said anxiously.

She quickly began assigning everyone a planet, except for Chris. She decided that he wasn't able to do the assignment, after all he always cried can't. This project would be no different from the other assignments given, Mrs. J cunningly thought.

Chris quickly raised his hand.

"Yes, Chris." said Mrs. J.

"I think you forgot to assign me a planet." He said.

"Well, Chris I kind of thought you couldn't do the assignment." Said Mrs. J.

"Oh no I love drawing and reading about the solar system!" He said eagerly.

"I'm sorry Chris, but I don't have a planet for you." She said.

"Okay." Chris sadly replied with his head down.

At that very moment Chris no longer liked feeling invisible.

That night, Chris sat in his room angry at Mrs. J and decided the perfect way to prove her wrong!

The next day after the last student presented their planet, Chris hurled his hand in the air like a rocket.

"Yes, Chris." Asked Mrs. J.

"I have something to share as well!" he said loudly.

Surprised, Mrs. J said well of course you can present. Chris walked to the front of the class carrying a handful of items and a huge grin.

He then took a deep breath and began speaking. "I've been working on this solar system collage for years now!" He said, as he placed it on the board for all to see.

Bright reds, blues, greens, and yellows were bursting all over! Each line was drawn to perfection making each planet look so real. It was a true outer space experience.

Everyone's eyes began to light up in amazement.

Chris then passed around his drawings. "Mrs. J I stayed up all night making these especially for our class!"

Wow, I am so happy you thought of us. Thank you Chris!" She said.

"Chris can you teach me how to draw these? Brian said.

No, me first! Said another student.

I want mine to look just like yours!" The entire class shouted.

"Yep, I sure can!" He said proudly.

Chris then walked back to the front of the class and stood for all to see him. He was victorious! He had finally done something without feeling embarrassed.

Waves of claps from everyone including Mrs. J flooded the room. They stood in true astonishment of Chris' abilities.

"I wasn't sure if you could do it Chris, but you were fantastic!" Said Mrs. J.

"Well, as you can see, I CAN Mrs. J, I CAN!" Chris repeated proudly.

Chris quickly became a natural in helping his classmates create eye popping pictures. It didn't take long for the classroom walls to begin filling up with tons of colorful drawings.

Later that week Mrs. J gathered the class to announce the grades received on the project. Chris took a big gulp as he listened.

"Class I am pleased to say that everyone did a marvelous job, but there was one student in particular that shined like the sun. Chris, you did an outstanding job and I am pleased to say you received an A+!" She said happily.

Chris had never smiled so hard!

For the first time Chris had finally told himself that he CAN do something and very well! Mrs. J always saw the CAN and knew it was only a matter of time that he would see it too. From that day forward Chris never again cried CAN'T.

"Sometimes it takes a special someone to see the CAN in us"-C.B.J

About the Author

Camesha B. Jackson has been in the education field for several years. Becoming an educator had always been a goal of hers since childhood. She is currently teaching at the elementary level. Her love for children and writing seemed to be second nature. The passion for writing and the arts were instilled at a very early age by family. At 10yrs old she had her first piece of writing published in the local town paper. It was at that moment she realized any and everything was possible.

Camesha obtained her Bachelors of Arts in English from Southern Illinois University-Carbondale and a Master of Arts in Elementary Education from Saint Xavier University. Her experience in working with a diverse group of students has truly been the fuel in driving the work completed thus far. She believes that "can't" doesn't exist and "can" will always be victorious in all things we set our minds to do.

"The can will always conquer the can't!" C.B.J

Made in the USA
Charleston, SC
30 August 2012